# I Want to
# Be a Pirate!

Licensed by The Illuminated Film Company
Based on the LITTLE PRINCESS animation series © The Illuminated Film Company 2008.
Made under licence by Andersen Press Ltd., London
'I Want to Be a Pirate!' episode written by Olly Smith.
Producer Iain Harvey. Director Edward Foster.
© The Illuminated Film Company/Tony Ross 2008.
Design and layout © Andersen Press Ltd, 2008.
Printed and bound in China.

10   9   8   7   6   5   4   3   2

British Library Cataloguing in Publication Data available.

ISBN: 978 1 84270 766 1

# I Want to
# Be a Pirate!

**Tony Ross**

Andersen Press · London

"A-harr!" cried the Little Princess. "I'm a pirate!"
The Little Princess's magnificent sea painting had
given her the idea.

She dug out a pointy umbrella sword, then pinged an old party hat onto her toy ted.

"Good parrot, Gilbert," she grinned.

The Little Princess checked her picture to see what else was needed. "I can't be a pirate without a proper pirate's hat."

"All hands on deck!" cried a voice outside.
The Princess peeped down at the Admiral. *He* definitely
had a proper pirate's hat!

The Admiral wasn't at all sure about handing
over his headgear.
"Pirates are very naughty people," he frowned.
"Never do what they're told."
The Little Princess thought for a moment,
then smiled sweetly. "I promise not to be a
really naughty pirate."

The Admiral couldn't resist any longer. The precious object was carefully placed on the Little Princess's head. "It's the best hat in the navy," he warned. "Never let her out of your sight."

"Thank you!" giggled the Little Princess.

The Little Pirate Princess was soon skipping across the castle garden. If she was going to be a proper pirate, she needed to get as far away as possible from the pond. "Sssshh!" she whispered. "I'm going to be naughty!"

"La la la la laaa!" trilled the Maid, hanging out the royal washing. The Little Princess chuckled cheekily, then dived behind a tree. As soon as the Maid's back was turned, she popped a surprise into the laundry basket. It was time to dish out some pirate treatment!

The Maid reached down for a sock.
"Waahh, frog!" she shrieked. "Princess?"
The scurvy young rascal had already run away.

The Little Pirate Princess chose the Chef as her next victim.

She crept on tiptoe into the kitchen, then bellowed,

# "BOO!"

The surprised Chef squirted icing all over his prize gateaux.

Nobody in the kingdom was safe. The Little Princess and her parrot sent the General's toy soldiers flying across the castle hallway, but she didn't care. She was a pirate!

The Little Princess swashbuckled her way outside,
then found a garden spade.
"I'm a pirate and I'm digging for treasure!" she announced.
The Little Princess peered into the muddy hole she had
made. There wasn't much treasure down there – in fact,
the only thing she could spot was a wiggly worm.
"I know!" she suddenly cried. "Pirates don't dig for
treasure, they steal it."
It was time to search the kingdom for some riches.

The General was just telling the Admiral about some
of the terrible things that the Little Princess had done,
when they got another shock.
"Are you there?" called out the Little Princess. "I've come
to steal your treasure!"

The Admiral thought it best to dive into the bulrushes.
"No treasure here," he mumbled. "Sorry, very busy!"
The Little Princess frowned. "I can't be a real pirate
without treasure."

"Princess! Lunchtime!" called the Maid.

"But I was just getting pirate treasure," pouted the Little Princess.

"Well now you can be a treasure and come inside."

The Little Princess grumpily turned her trike round.
"I bet real pirates don't get told what to do."

The Admiral and the General waited until the pirate had
pedalled back up to the castle door before they issued the
all-clear.

"Aharr, me hearties!" roared the Little Princess, as she entered the living-room.

"Hello, poppet," nodded the King.

"Go and wash your hands then, sweetheart," smiled the Queen.

The Little Princess shook her head and sat down.

"Pirates are naughty, they don't have to wash. And they only eat proper pirate food."

The King and Queen swapped glances, then turned to the Chef.

"*Voilà!*" cried the Chef with a flourish.

"Real food for a real pirate!"

The Little Princess gasped in horror.

"Cold fish stew," added the Queen.

The Chef waltzed back into the room with two delicious plates
of sausage and mash.

"Yummy," chuckled the King, as he tucked in.

The Little Princess frowned. "I don't think I like pirate food
very much."

After lunch, the Maid agreed to have a game of
pirates. "We'll ride the high seas, me hearty!"
The Little Princess grinned and nodded frantically.
"But first we have to swab the deck," said the Maid.

Scrubbing the castle steps was not the type of
adventure the Little Princess had in mind.

"Is this really what pirates do?" she asked.

"Aye, aye!" cried the Maid. "Especially the naughty ones!"

The Little Princess escaped to the
garden as quickly as she could.
"Let's go and find some buried treasure!"
suggested the Gardener.

But after ten minutes, the Little Princess gave up.

"This isn't pirate treasure, it's potatoes!"

"They're my treasure," beamed the Gardener. "Only four barrows to go, shipmate."

The Little Princess dropped her spade. "That's it! This is no fun."

"I don't like being a pirate!" sighed the Little Princess. She lifted the Admiral's hat up, then tore off her eyepatch. "Pirates eat yucky food and do really hard work, it's horrible!" she sobbed. "And my eye patch is really itchy."

Worst of all, nobody wanted to play with a naughty pirate.
It was time to go and find the Admiral and the General.

The Little Princess gently floated the Admiral's hat
back across the pond.
"I don't want to be a pirate any more!" she whispered.
"Sorry if I was too naughty."

The Admiral chuckled as he reached for his hat.

"It's good to have you back, Princess," smiled the General.

"What shall we play now then?" asked the Admiral.

The Little Princess clapped her hands. "Oooh! I know...

...naughty sea monsters!"